Friendship Rules

Amadeus
The Traveling Dog

Published and distributed by

Legacy Publishers

division of Evaluation Enterprises, Inc.
2386 Clower Street, Building G, Suite 101
Snellville, GA 30078-6134
Information and Orders: 1.800.290.8055 or 770.979.7899
E-mail: Legacy@eeinc.org
http://www.eeinc.org

Printed in Canada
ISBN 1-932957-00-6

First Printing

This book is dedicated to my friend

Chris Cofer

My name is Amadeus. You say it like this: "Ah-muh-day-us."
I am a Great Pyrenees Mountain Dog.
I am a Certified Canine Good Citizen with the American Kennel Club.

Please visit my website at
http://www.eeinc.org/amadeus/
amadeusbooks.com

This books belongs to:

Vestavia Hills Library

This is my right, front paw.
(I have fluffy white fur between my toes).

Amadeus
The Traveling Dog

One fine, sunny spring-like day,
 a funny-looking hat came my way.
What was that?
Was it really a hat?
Is there something in the hat?
"I must take a closer look," I say.

It could be a hat.
It could be a sack.
It could be a bag,
   or even a gag.

I poked my head inside to see.
What a surprise was waiting for me!

7

A tiny kitten was looking back at me.
A kitten in a hat?
"Why is that?"
I asked the kitten,
    who was staring right back.

"Meow," said a voice.
"Good day to you, sir.

What else is such a
        small kitten to do, sir?

I have no home,
        so I snuggle in here.
It's really quite cozy
        and full of good cheer."

The kitten was cute.
The kitten was fuzzy.
But she was not a real
        kitten, was she?

9

I turned around and to my surprise,
A beautiful cat was looking right into my eyes.
In a soft voice she said, "I'm Penny Kitty.
My friends call me Penny because my eyes are so pretty.
They are round and the color of a one-cent penny."

"Hello, Penny." I said with a smile.
"My name is Amadeus. Can you stay for a while?"
Penny was afraid. I could tell right away.
But I was very gentle because I wanted her to stay.

11

The next thing I saw to my surprise, was three copper-colored cats.
I couldn't believe my eyes.
"This is my family," said Penny the Cat.
"We've been living here, right under this great big hat.
Either I am getting bigger or the hat is getting small.
Soon there won't be room in this hat for us all."

I wanted to help the kitten feel safe,
  so I laid down beside her and tried not to chase.
Dogs are known to chase cats, it's true.
But this dog and this cat are friends, true blue.

"You can live with me,"
  I told the cat.
"You will no longer
  have to live in a hat."

We got her a perch,
  so she can climb very high.
Cats like to do that,
  I don't know why.

"What will we do with the hat?"
  Penny asked.
"Finding a good use for it
  will be a fine task."

14

"I've got it," I laughed
   as I put the big hat on my head.
"I'll wear the funny hat
   that is striped white and red."

Now I'm a dog in a hat.
How funny is that?
Is it funnier than a cat in a hat?

"Let's play with this toy,"
I said to the baby cat.
"We can have fun doing things like that."

"I'll roll it to you.
Then you roll it to me.
We can chase it together.
It will be fun, you'll see."

We rolled the toy here.
We rolled the toy there.
Then the toy rolled under a chair!
Oops!

The chair was too small for me to fit under.
Could Penny, that wee little kitten, get the toy?
I wondered.

Penny was small.
She could fit anywhere.
She happily crawled under that chair.

Quick as a wink
    she had that toy out.
She did such a good job
I wanted to shout.
"Hurray for Penny!
The hero of the day.
She saved our game,"
I wanted to say.

18

And I did say it,
  for all the world to hear.
"Woof, woof," I said.
Tiny kittens can sometimes do
  what a large dog
  would never dare.

They have special skills,
  these small creatures do.
That's what I think.
How about you?"

"Mew, mew," said Penny
as polite as can be.
"I am just glad that
I could set the toy free."

20

"It makes me happy,"
said the small cat.
"To be so helpful
with jobs like that."

21

Penny said, "Thank you, Amadeus, for being my friend.

Now, I am the happiest kitten there ever has been."

Penny and I became friends fast.
We have a friendship that will last.
We made ten rules that are nice to know.
They will help our friendship grow.

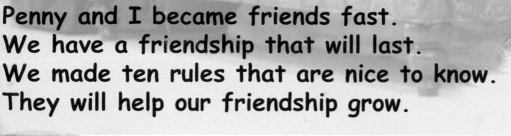 is for Feelings.

We do not hurt each other's feelings
by saying hurtful words.
Talking mean is for the birds!

 is for Respect.

I treat Penny the way
    I want her to treat me.
That is what everyone should do.
It is plain to see.

 is for Interest.

Penny and I are interested in
    each other's moods.
That helps each of us know when
    the other is feeling bad,
    or feeling good.

E is for Ears.

Ears are for listening.
You might as well know.
Listening to each other.
That is the smart way to go.

 is for nice.

I talk nicely to Penny,
   and she talks nicely to me.

Being nice does not cost anything.
It is free.

D is for Disagree.

Penny and I agree;
  that sometimes it is all right
  for us to disagree.

27

S is for Share.

Penny and I share
    stories, ideas, and even toys.
This is a good idea
    for all girls and boys.

h is for Help.

I always help Penny
when a problem comes up.

I know that she will
do the same for this pup.

I is for individual.

Each person is different,
that we all know.
We must give each other room,
to be ourselves as we grow.

30

P is for Playmate.

Be the kind of playmate
you want your friends to be.
That will make you both
very happy.

Each letter in the word Friendship
stands for one rule.

Let's spell the word now,

F-R-I-E-N-D-S-H-I-P.
Now wasn't that cool?

FRIENDSHIP

You can learn the rules
   by practicing them each day.
Put them on your wall,
   and remember them when you play.

Draw a picture of how the rules
   help you be a better friend.
When friends use the rules,
   they all win.

Penny is fun.
She is feisty and more.
She is full of energy,
  and she is not a bore.
Penny is a friend that
  I have come to adore.

34

I was lucky that sunny day that it happened.
The day I met a cat who was hattin'.
Hattin' is a new word I made up myself,
   to describe what Penny was doing hiding in
   that great big hat like an elf.

Penny and I still use
our 10 Friendship Rules.

We hope you will find
them helpful too.

The End

36